THE
SEA
TIGER

For Neil

First U.S. edition 2015

Library of Congress Catalog Card Number 2014952641
ISBN 978-0-7636-7986-6

15 16 17 18 19 20 TTP 10 9 8 7 6 5 4 3 2 1

Printed in Huizhou, Guangdong, China

This book was typeset in Tenebra, Cochin, Providence, and Minion Pro.
The illustrations were done in colored pencil.

Edited by Katie Cotton
Designed by Mike Jolley

TEMPLAR BOOKS

an imprint of
Candlewick Press
99 Dover Street
Somerville, Massachusetts 02144
www.candlewick.com

THE SEA TIGER

VICTORIA TURNBULL

templar books

an imprint of Candlewick Press

I am the Sea Tiger.

And this is Oscar.

I am Oscar's best friend. We do everything together.

Where I lead, Oscar follows.

We go to extraordinary places.

We have so much

fun together.

Anything is possible.

After a day full of

adventure, we're

ready for bed.

Sometimes
we
fall
straight
to
sleep.

Sometimes I have to

scare the monsters away.

And sometimes,
for no particular
reason, we hitch
a ride to
the surface . . .

and look out at the sky

studded with stars.

I am Oscar's best friend.

I am Oscar's only friend.

Where I lead, Oscar follows.

That's why it's up to me . . .

to make a new friend . . .

so that Oscar can too.